For the Aldrich family and all of Santa's helpers
—Denise

To all of Santa's helpers, who keep the magic alive
—Deborah

Library of Congress Cataloging-in-Publication Data

Printed and bound in the United States.
10 9 8 7 6 5 4 3 2 1

Names: Brennan-Nelson, Denise, author. | Melmon, Deborah, illustrator.

Title: Santa's secret / written by Denise Brennan-Nelson ; illustrated by Deborah Melmon.

Description: Ann Arbor, MI : Sleeping Bear Press, [2019] | Summary: A young detective is determined
to uncover which of the Santas he sees in the big city is the one and only Santa Claus.

Identifiers: LCCN 2019010250 | ISBN 9781534110380 (hardcover)

Subjects: | CYAC: Stories in rhyme. | Santa Claus—Fiction. |

Christmas—Fiction. | Mystery and detective stories.

Classification: LCC PZ8.3.B7457 San 2019 | DDC [E]—dc23

LC record available at https://lccn.loc.gov/2019010250

SANTA'S SECRET

By Denise Brennan-Nelson ❀ Illustrated by Deborah Melmon

PUBLISHED BY SLEEPING BEAR PRESS

My parents had planned an adventure one day.
We loaded the car and went on our way.

We sang Christmas carols to Grandma's delight,
Till we got to the city, all festive and bright.

and a partridge in a pear tree...

The sidewalks were packed, but we made our way through,
And I climbed on Dad's shoulders to get the best view.

A holiday parade was soon underway,
With marching bands playing and floats on display.

Santa came into sight and the cheering grew loud.
From a shiny red sleigh, he waved to the crowd.

When the parade ended, we walked for a while,
And who did we see with a bell and a smile?

Ring Ring

He wore the same suit, but I knew right away
He wasn't the Santa I had seen in the sleigh.

"That's not the same Santa!"
I loudly declared.
The people nearby
turned toward me
and stared.

Mama said, "Santa needs helpers to get the job done."
But I demanded to know: "Who is the REAL one?!"

Grandma leaned down with an answer for me—
"It's Santa's secret, just as it should be."

But everyone knows that secrets want out.
I'd uncover the truth; I hadn't a doubt.

We found Santa's Station and waited in line
Until finally, thank goodness, the next turn was mine.

His beard was as white as fresh-fallen snow.
And his belly jiggled with each "Ho, Ho, Ho!"

I had questions for Santa. I would see what he knew—
About reindeer and elves and the rest of the crew.

I got out my notebook. I would crack this case wide!
From a good detective, the truth cannot hide.

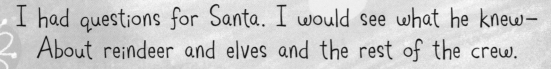

TOYS!

WINTER
CATALOG

HOW TO
BE A
GOOD
LISTENER

Peppermint
BEARD
OIL

FIRST AID

Breath
Mints

"What is your name?" I started off simple.
On each side of his grin, I noticed a dimple.

PASSPORT
North Pole
EARTH

Name: Santa Claus
aka: Old St. Nick
Father Christmas
Kris Kringle

Dasher Dancer Prancer Vixen Comet Cupid Donner Blitzen

Who are your reindeer? What do they eat?
And does Rudolph have a favorite treat?

Do your reindeer sleep?

Rudolph

North Pole
Reindeer Barn
Workshop
Sleigh Parking

Where do you live?

Who helps you decide
what presents to give?

Do you like to fly? Do you take vacations?
Tell me a few of your favorite locations.

How big is your workshop and how many elves?
Do they live with you or all by themselves?

Well some of the elves live with me I know there are a few who live in the village & commute to work

I had to be thorough to get to the truth.
I recorded his answers like any great sleuth.

I paused for a moment and looked into his eyes—
This question would catch him by surprise:

Santa Claus chuckled, and his reply
Was a tug of his beard and a wink of his eye.

Then he patted my head and had a question for me:
"What is it you'd like beneath your tree?"

I thought my investigation should persist,
But I thanked him instead and gave him my list.

We then settled in to a warm coffee shop—
Hot cocoa for me, with marshmallows on top!

Looking over my notes—did I have enough?
Could I solve this case or was it too tough?

But then catching my eye, tucked back in a nook,
Sitting all by himself, reading a book—

Was a man with a beard. His coat on the chair.
Weathered black boots . . . I couldn't help but stare.

He munched on a cookie and sipped on a drink.
There was something about him; I didn't dare blink.

With notepad in hand, "Excuse me," I said.
I saw that his cheeks were bright cherry red.

His smile stretched up and crinkled his eyes,
And then without asking, to my surprise—

He said, "Reindeer like barley and berries to eat."
"But carrots," he added, "are their favorite treat."

I turned toward Mama for a second, I swear!
And when I turned back, the man wasn't there.

I had seen a few Santas throughout the day.
Had I met the real one? This sleuth cannot say.

Grandma is right, it's "as it should be."
So I'll keep Santa's secret. It's safe with me.

The End